PRAISE FOR DAEDALUS

A strange thing happened to me while reading Robert G. Williscroft's story *Daedalus*: I felt it hard to believe it was fiction. Earlier, I had read his novel *Slingshot* about the world's first Space Launch Loop, and since *Daedalus* follows it, I should have known it was fiction. Still, this hard science-fiction tale is told with such vivid, realistic, sometimes visceral detail and moment-by-moment suspense that I almost completely lost myself in it. When I finished the story, I felt I had shared Derek "Tiger" Baily's harrowing flight in his *Gryphon-7* wingsuit.

Why is Derek risking his life? Simple: they need to test the limits of *Gryphon-7*, which is "an entirely new kind of weapon, or perhaps *delivery system*." Carried above by the Space Loop, he falls in his full-body, fuel-supplied spacesuit 80,000 meters toward the Earth. He is a true pioneer, the first to attempt this journey, and there are unexpected surprises and dangers along the way. Don't miss the ride!

— Professor John B. Rosenman, Norfolk State University
Former Chairman of the Board, Horror Writers Association
Author of *The Inspector of the Cross Series*

Afraid of Heights?

Then you won't make it as a member of SEAL Winged Insertion Command.

For a once in a lifetime thrill, follow the thoughts and actions of Derek "Tiger" Bailey, most adept member of Second Platoon, First Squad as he wrings out the details of making a wingsuit jump from a platform eighty kilometers (fifty miles) above Jarvis Island on the Equator in the middle of the Pacific Ocean. Tiger Bailey reached that platform using the "Slingshot" space portal system described in Robert G. Williscroft's richly detailed series of hard science fiction novels, *The Starchild Trilogy*. But rather than launch into space from the Fred Noonan Skyport, Tiger Bailey attempts a 236-mile traverse over the ever threatening and oh-so-deep ocean waters. This is what SEALs do, test new means of surreptitiously inserting themselves into combat zones.

While the beginning and middle of Williscroft's short story are mesmerizing, the fifty-mile high drop and long distance transit will have you holding your breath.

Much to Williscroft's credit, the physics and dynamics of Tiger's record-breaking flight seem spot on.

This story won't take you long to read, but I promise you'll keep thinking about it for a long time.

– Dr. John R. Clarke
Author of *The Jason Parker Series*

Williscroft's usual attention to technical detail and firsthand experience with military ops pays off in this wild tale set in the world of his *Slingshot*, about the first wingsuit jump from a launch loop.

– Alastair Mayer
Author of *The T-Space Series*

Daedalus is a science fiction short story that blends the boundaries of fact and fiction as seamlessly as the late master, Michael Crichton. It's the type of story that leaves you asking questions and discussing with your coworkers in the break room. The story is told by Derek "Tiger" Baily, a member of an elite SEAL team who completes the first jump in an experimental wingsuit from a skyport 80 km above the Earth. Now, if you've read *Slingshot*, a full-length sci-fi thriller published by Williscroft a few years ago (see my review—5 stars for this well-crafted and thought-provoking story) you'll know all about the skyport, a marvel of engineering that could be close to being realized (really!). And if you haven't read *Slingshot*, no worries because an excerpt is thoughtfully included at the end of *Daedalus*.

Tiger is a self-professed adrenalin junkie who doesn't shy away from a challenge. I won't share any spoilers here, because it is best to allow yourself to become one with Tiger as he flies his wingsuit to his target landing zone – a tiny atoll in the Pacific Ocean. What begins as a normal drop soon turns into a terrifying descent into Nature's fury that will leave you in a cold sweat.

Is *Daedalus* fact or fiction? I'll leave it to you to decide. Oh, and pick up *The Starchild Trilogy* – but be prepared to have your world turned on edge!

– Dr. Dave Edlund
***USA Today* Bestselling Author –**
The Peter Savage Thrillers

DAEDALUS

SWIC Basejump from Fred Noonan Skyport

DAEDALUS

SWIC Basejump from Fred Noonan Skyport

Robert G. Williscroft

Fresh Ink Group
Guntersville

DAEDALUS
SWIC Basejump from Fred Noonan Skyport

Fresh Ink Group
An Imprint of:
The Fresh Ink Group, LLC
Box 931
Guntersville, AL 35976
info@FreshInkGroup.com
FreshInkGroup.com

Edition 1.0 2019

Cover art by Anik / FIG
Artwork by Robert G. Williscroft
Book design by Amit Dey / FIG
Covers by Stephen Geez / FIG

BISAC Subject Headings:
FIC028020 FICTION / Science Fiction / Hard Science Fiction
FIC002000 FICTION / Action & Adventure
FIC028010 FICTION / Science Fiction / Action & Adventure

Library of Congress Control Number: 2019941739

ISBN-13:
978-1-947867-56-7 Papercover
978-1-947867-57-4 Hardcover
978-1-947867-58-1 Ebooks

DEDICATION

This story is dedicated to parachute record-holder Alan Eustace, to Wingsuit Flyers Dean Potter and Graham Hunt, and to the World Wingsuit community.

TABLE OF CONTENTS

ACKNOWLEDGMENTS

Several people contributed to the creation of this book.

Most significantly, my wonderful wife, Jill, whom I first met when I returned from a year at the South Pole conducting atmospheric research, and who finally consented to marry me nearly thirty years later, pored over this story with her discerning engineer's eye. She kept my timeline honest, and made sure that regular readers could understand fully the arcane details of the Launch Loop and the Gryphon.

Jill's twin sons, Arthur and Robert, also read the manuscript, and provided their insights.

Hard science fiction authors Alastair Mayer, John Clark, and Prof. John Rosenman, and USA Today bestselling author Dave Edlund reviewed the manuscript and offered their editorial insights.

Lauren Smith from Fresh Ink Group applied her professional associate publisher's eyes to improve the story.

It goes without saying that any remaining omissions, errors, and mistakes fall directly on my shoulders.

Robert G. Williscroft, PhD
Centennial, Colorado
June 2019

FOREWORD

Slingshot is my novel about constructing the world's first Space Launch Loop. The inventor of the concept, Keith Lofstrom, wrote the foreword to that novel. Here is a portion of that Foreword.

> Imagine a stream of water out of a fire hose. Without air friction, the stream might make a parabolic arc 20 meters high. Faster, and the arc goes higher and farther. A stream moving 7.3 kilometers per second would come down on the other side of the planet, and a stream moving 11 kilometers per second would keep going into interplanetary space. Wrap the stream in a frictionless hose, and...THAT won't work either. But what if...?
>
> The launch loop: replace the water with flexible iron pipe, 5 centimeters outer diameter, 3 metric tons per kilometer, moving at 14 kilometers per second. Bend it to the curvature of the earth with a stationary magnetic track, 7 metric tons per kilometer, 2,000 kilometers long, at 80 kilometers altitude. Stabilize the moving iron with electromagnets controlled by fast electronics. Turn it around at the ends with powerful magnets, and complete the loop.
>
> On the eastbound section, 5-metric-ton payloads ride on magnets designed for high drag, which accelerates payloads at 3 gees. Payloads exit the east end of the track between 7.7 and 11 kilometers per second, to equatorial low earth orbits, to the moon, or to interplanetary space. Launching a payload weighing 5 metric tons to low earth orbit consumes 180 megawatt-hours, about $15,000 worth of electricity, or $3 per kilogram

of payload. Passengers will still need vehicles and air, but freight can be launched on wooden shipping pallets. This small launch loop can launch 2,000 5-metric-ton payloads to orbit per day. Heavier launch loops can launch thousands of standard 30-metric-ton intermodal shipping containers per hour. They can also store peak power for the global electrical grid. Space travel can be as cheap as ocean cargo travel.

In the early 1980s, I published in an *American Astronautical Society Newsletter* and other journals, and presented at many conferences. In England, physicist Paul Birch wrote about orbital rings in the *Journal of the British Interplanetary Society*. Ken Brakke, a math professor in Pennsylvania, published his version of orbital rings.

Ken, Paul, and I met at one of the Space Studies Institute conferences at Princeton. We spent three days developing nomenclature, doing math, finding errors and fixes. I met Robert Williscroft in the mid-1990s in Philadelphia while I was on a trip to the East Coast. He had contacted me about a novel he was outlining – *Slingshot*. We spent a day together becoming acquainted and have kept in touch since then. *Slingshot* in its current form is a result of our brainstorming during that visit.

For years afterwards, Paul and I swapped ideas. Under Jerome Pearson's leadership, and with our friend John Knapman, we submitted grant proposals until Paul's untimely passing in 2012. We were friends, never competitors, though Paul was much better at reciting Tennyson. I hope one of us will be the first launch loop astronaut. Conflict makes great stories, but friendship makes great lives, so I now pass page control to my friend R.G....

So there you have it. I wrote *Slingshot*. It was launched at the International Space Elevator Conference in Seattle in August 2015, and the book resides on the desk of every Space Elevator scientist in the world. Space

Launch Loops appear in the subsequent books in *The Starchild Trilogy*, and anyone familiar with my *Trilogy* knows all about these commercial space launch systems.

When I discovered the *Gryphon* rigid wingsuit, the story you are about to read pushed itself into my consciousness. It's the natural consequence of Slingshot's skyports effectively being 80 km tall towers.

Robert G. Williscroft Centennial,
Colorado
June 2019

CAST OF CHARACTERS

SEAL Winged Insertion Command Three (SWIC-3)

Lt. Brad Nelson – Officer-in-Charge of Second Platoon.
Lt. Tom Spitzer – Executive Officer Second Platoon.
Senior Chief Jerry Boldt – In charge of Second Platoon, First Squad.
Derek "Tiger" Baily – Narrator, member of Second Platoon, First Squad.

Launch Loop International (LLI)

Apryl Searson – Diver EMT.

DAEDALUS

CALIFORNIA – SEVERAL YEARS IN THE PAST

Obviously, I survived, since I am telling this story. But it's not that simple – let me explain.

My name is Derek Baily. I'm an extreme sports enthusiast, an adrenaline junkie. It all started several years ago when I made my first parachute jump. Before that, I was just your typical skateboarder, snowboarder, trick-bike rider…I think you get the idea. I had gone parasailing a couple of times, and it was really cool. I decided I wanted to do more of that, and was talking it over with my buds.

That's when one of them suggested that I try a jump. "Jump out of a perfectly safe airplane?" I asked, but only half in jest.

"How about next Saturday?" he said.

YOSEMITE PARK – TWO YEARS LATER

One thing led to another, and a couple of years later, on May 16, I found myself standing on Taft Point in Yosemite National Park, dressed in a fire-engine-red wingsuit. It wasn't as if I had permission or anything, it was just something I had to do. I was there to commemorate the ill-fated flight of Dean Potter and Graham Hunt from the same spot on the same day back in 2015. A couple of Forest Rangers with a bullhorn did their very best to stop me. They had followed me to the Point, and were perhaps three meters away, and I still wasn't quite ready – I mean I still had to narrow my focus. But it was then or never, so I jumped.

The first hundred meters were a bit rough as I got my act together. I would have flipped off the Rangers, but my hands were kinda full. My wingsuit was significantly better than was Potter's. He had a three-to-one glide ratio – better than most, but not quite good enough to hit the slot that loomed ahead of me. It could have been a down-draft that got him and Hunt, but I think they cut it a bit too close. I had a glide ratio of five-to-one, which meant hitting the slot was a piece of cake. I cleared it by about a meter-and-a- half, with clear flying beyond. I stretched it out as long as possible, and finally popped my canopy as close to the ground as I dared – maybe a hundred meters or so. I landed standing, soft as a feather. By the time the Rangers got there, my pickup crew and I were long gone.

Like I said, that's how I got from there to here.

CORONADO, CALIFORNIA – THE GRYPHON

The worldwide wingsuit community is quite small, although it has grown in the last few decades. Even so, there were less than a thousand of us – that is until the military figured out how to turn our sport into a pretty nifty weapon system with a little help from the Special Parachute and Logistics Consortium (SPELCO) in Germany. SPELCO had built an experimental wingsuit called the *Gryphon* that, in its original version, had a glide ratio of five-to-one – when everything else was between two-and-a- half and three to one. It was pretty exciting, except no one could afford one. It turned out the Navy SEAL Teams picked up on the concept, and quietly developed a combat model.

Someone in the SEAL hierarchy concluded it might be useful to recruit guys from the wingsuit community. They even put together a special program that bypassed regular boot camp and all the other stuff a guy normally goes through before being assigned to BUDS – Basic Underwater Demolition/SEAL training. About a year after I shot the slot in Yosemite, I found myself in Coronado, California, training with a bunch of the toughest bad-asses I had ever met. BUDS was the hardest thing I ever did, literally, absolutely! Somehow I made it through. Don't ask me how I did it, because I don't have a clue. I just put one foot in front of the other, raised my arms for one more stroke in the surf, dug down and found another push-up…I just slogged along, firmly believing I was sucking hind tit, barely surviving, hoping against hope that I would make it through.

As it turned out, to my total astonishment, I was one of the top guys in my class. Beyond BUDS, I went through a whole series of advanced training scenarios. Even though I had been recruited specifically for my wingsuit background, the SEALs insisted that I undergo the entire training cycle. Two years later – yeah, that's right, a full two years later – I finally reported to my new outfit, the SEAL Winged Insertion Command, SWIC for short.

SWIC was a team unto itself, filling a new slot in the Naval Special Warfare Group Five hierarchy. It consisted of three teams. SWIC-1 covered the Pacific and Middle East, SWIC-2 covered Europe, the Med, and Africa, and SWIC-3 covered worldwide. SWIC-1 and 3 were based in Coronado, and SWIC-2 was in Norfolk. I was assigned to Second Platoon in SWIC-3. Lt. Brad Nelson was in charge, and his second was Lt. Tom Spitzer. I was in First Squad run by Senior Chief Jerry Boldt. My platoon was working closely with SPELCO developing the latest incarnation of the *Gryphon*.

The *Gryphon* was a one-man unit that enabled a person to "fly," the only thing it still had in common with the wingsuits I had flown. The old wingsuits were really nothing more than a suit with fabric filling the gaps between stretched out arms and ankles, and between the legs. The *Gryphon* was a carapace that you strapped on your body. It stopped short of your feet, but in flight could extend to a full two meters, stretching beyond your feet. It attached to the legs and arms, with special controls for each hand, and had a broad Velcro band across the midriff. It had extensible delta wings with a three-meter wingspan.

The back end contained a small steerable hypergolic rocket engine, and the left and right wings each contained pressurized hypergolic fuel components. Switches in the hand units controlled the fuel valves. The *Gryphon* had a heads-up display with height-over-ground, airspeed, groundspeed, compass, and GPS coordinates superimposed on a map, plus various system readouts.

Here is the really amazing thing about these suckers. When I flew my old wingsuits, I had to pop a chute at about 300 meters, certainly no less than 100, because their typical airspeed was between 180 and 260 kilometers per hour that I needed to shed before landing. When flying a *Gryphon*, I can land with the same light touch I get from my best sport parachute.

CORONADO, CALIFORNIA – GRYPHON DROPS

Lt. Nelson had us make hundreds of drops from aircraft, coming in for soft landings. After each drop, under Nelson's close supervision, we would adjust this, change that, and then see how the modifications worked in another drop. Every now and again, one of us would have to deploy his emergency chute, because a particular modification screwed things up. Nelson was cool when this happened, but we could tell that his concern skyrocketed. Generally, however, we improved with every drop, much to the lieutenant's satisfaction. In a static drop, the *Gryphon* had a glide ratio of ten-to-one. That meant we could deploy at 3,000 meters and land thirty klicks away – soundlessly. Without fuel, the *Gryphon* could be collapsed and rolled into a one-and-a-half-meter-long roll that weighed just a few kilos and could be stowed easily, or even carried across the back. With fuel, if you still had some left after landing, it was just a bit bulkier, but still eminently man- transportable.

With the hypergolic rocket and full tanks, the *Gryphon* could fly horizontally for thirty klicks. A standing launch from the ground used up about a klick of fuel, but a launch from any height over ten meters gave you the full thirty. Climbing consumed fuel quickly, but a powered drop extended the horizontal range by thirty klicks.

With Lt. Nelson, mother-henning us all the way, we worked our way up to a 10,000-meter drop, carrying oxygen, of course. To put things into perspective, that's about 1,200 meters higher than Mt. Everest. Once we were comfortable doing this (but don't kid yourself, it never got routine) we set up for a 15,000-meter drop – from a balloon. Everyone in my squad volunteered, but I got chosen, probably because of my extensive prior wingsuit experience.

I'm not going to spend a lot of your time with the details of that drop. The thinner air in the initial minutes dropped my glide ratio way down, so I compensated with the rocket to generate some significant forward motion. When my groundspeed reached about 200, I secured the motor, and shortly found enough air to regain my ten-to- one. Basically, that was it. I landed nearly 150 klicks away without further rocket use. Since I had a bit of trouble determining my rate of descent, we added a descent-rate meter to the heads-up display for follow-on drops to what now was the *Gryphon (Mk 7-Mod 1)* – or just *Gryphon-7* for short. After that, Nelson let each squad member make the balloon drop, all without incident.

I know you have never heard of any of this, but you have to understand that this was all top-secret stuff. We were developing ways to drop into an enemy's presence with total surprise, take care of business, and be gone before they knew what hit them. You don't want to advertise that kind of capability.

❋

In 2014, Google mucky-muck Alan Eustace stepped into the record books with a parachute drop from 41,419 meters, reaching a falling velocity of 1,322 kph – that's Mach 1.1. If you are not impressed by that, you should be! Since there didn't seem to be any reason to better this, his record has stood the test of time.

The Teams had no reason to bring down the Eustace records; after all, that's not what we're about. But, we were nearly halfway there, and I would be lying if I told you we didn't talk about it. We were pretty sure, however, that Naval Special Warfare Group Five had no intentions of spending its tight budget on an exotic balloon. So...I'm not sure why we didn't see it coming. Blame our narrow focus on the immediate job at hand. We let the senior officers handle the big picture.

EQUATORIAL PACIFIC — SLINGSHOT

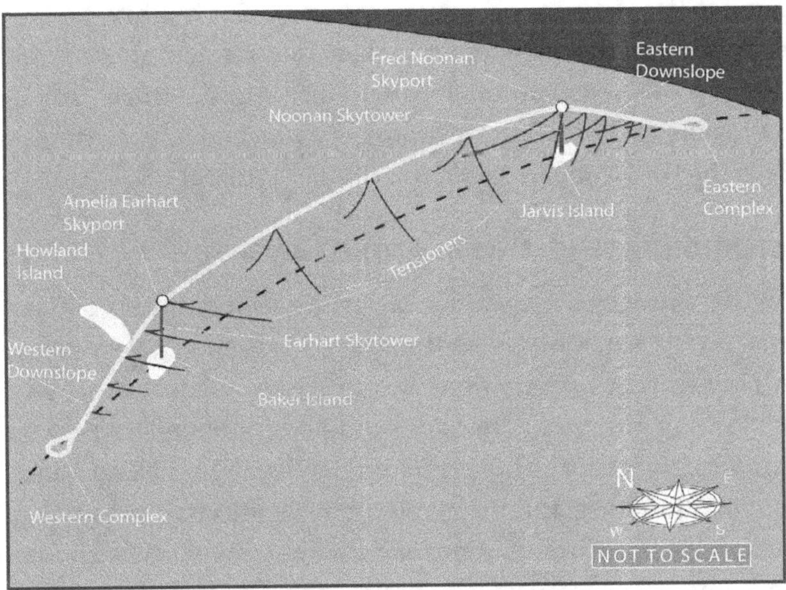

The Slingshot Space Launch Loop

I have to interrupt this tale to bring you up to speed on *Slingshot*. Yeah, I know, some of you already know all about the new Space Launch Loop stretching between Baker and Jarvis Islands in the equatorial Pacific. For the rest of you, try to visualize a five-centimeter-diameter soft- iron tube moving at nearly twelve kps, enclosed in a slightly larger stationary tube that starts a few meters below the ocean surface about 350 klicks west of Baker Island, rises to eighty klicks, and follows the curvature of the Earth for about 1,800 klicks to Jarvis Island, and then descends to a Complex east of Jarvis that is a mirror-image of the Complex to the west of Baker – and then it turns around and does the entire thing again in reverse. Now picture two elevator-like skytowers that connect each island to a skyport eighty klicks overhead. Stabilizing tensioners attached between the tube and ocean bottom maintain stability for the entire gossamer structure.

And here's the kicker. You get into a capsule on Baker Island, ride the skytower to the Amelia Earhart Skyport, attach magnetically to the rail (what they call the tube) just like an earthbound Maglev train, and several minutes later you are on your way to high Earth orbit, the Moon, or wherever, without the thundering rockets that we had to use until just a few years ago. Or…instead of launching into space, you can stay on the rail, slow yourself down with kick thrusters attached to your capsule, and debark at the Fred Noonan Skytower over Jarvis Island.

EQUATORIAL PACIFIC – HOWLAND ISLAND

And that's exactly what we did, Lt. Nelson, Senior Chief Boldt, and me and my six squadmates. Once again, I was the chosen jumper. No matter how you cut it, every time we did this, as the first choice, I racked up additional points, so that my stock-in-trade continued to grow over my squad mates. Not that they really minded. When it was all said and done, we were in it together, and they would get their turns – presuming I survived – with the benefit of my jump and the improvements I suggested. The goal this time, as you may have figured, was a *Gryphon* jump from 80,000 meters, with a 379-klick horizontal flight northeast to Kiritimati Island. The plan called for me to arrive on Kiritimati with twenty-five klicks of fuel left. Lt. Nelson and Senior Chief Boldt would monitor me by Link all the way, and we had comms available, although we did not really know how much back- and-forth we would have.

Anyway, we landed at Amelia Earhart International Airport on Howland Island just a few klicks north of the Equator and Baker Island. The sky was filled with thousands of birds – mostly sooty terns, lesser frigatebirds, and masked boobies, I was told. The guys running the show had found a way to keep the birds away from incoming and outgoing aircraft, but otherwise, they were everywhere. It was pretty amazing. The folks here told me that the eco- terrorists who tried to bring down *Slingshot* somehow got the idea that it was an ecological hazard. From everything I could see, however, there are more birds now, more fish now, and we can get to space without dumping thousands of tons of pollutants into the air. The way I add it up, everybody wins.

EQUATORIAL PACIFIC – BAKER ISLAND

Our transit to Baker was just like so many other Chinook rides we had made over the past several years, except for the birds. They flew the distance with us and seemed to avoid the rotary wings instinctively. Once we landed, a bus took us to the Socket Complex where we were briefed on the lightweight spacesuits we would wear. Launch Loop International (LLI) management wanted their own medical people to examine us – CYA, I guess. So, we were examined by this diver-EMT chick, Apryl Searson, who somehow managed to be both professional and beguiling simultaneously. I think everyone on my squad hit on her, but she reminded us that in a few minutes we would be some 2,000 klicks to the east, and she had better things to do than wait around for some horny sailors – even if they were SEALS. Nevertheless, when Apryl finished examining me, she stood on her tiptoes and whispered in my ear, "Good luck, Tiger!" followed by a fleeting kiss. Go figure! My heart rate must have hit 140, and the name stuck! The guys have been calling me *Tiger* ever since.

We donned our suits, carried our transparent globular helmets, and trudged toward the launch area. The capsule looked like a small, streamlined, light-rail car. Gull-wing doors that exposed the entire inside of the capsule opened on the left side. We slipped into memory-foam seats that accommodated us beautifully, and strapped in with over-the-shoulder harnesses that snapped in our laps. The nine of us, counting Lt. Nelson, fit into the capsule just fine, but the Socket Controller wouldn't let us take the wing with us, because of its hypergolic fuel load.

"Don't worry," he said. "It'll follow by five minutes in a freight capsule."

The trip up was exhilarating. Shortly after we tilted to vertical, I felt a faint tug that rapidly increased to about the same pressure produced by a chick sitting on my chest. I could just hear the high-pitched whine of the gyrostabilizer in the back. I heard an extended whoosh and turned my head to see fleecy clouds whip past the window. Seventeen seconds later (I counted them), and eight kilometers above the ground, the capsule shuddered. "Passing the sound barrier," a soft woman's voice floated through the capsule from concealed speakers. A few seconds later, the weight on my chest decreased slowly until I felt completely normal. Back to one gee. The capsule shuddered again, accompanied by a clank as the capsule shifted from the boost cable to the lift cable. The whooshing faded as the capsule, rising at more than 400 meters per second, left most of the Earth's air behind as it entered the rarified air of the upper stratosphere. There was no vibration, no sense of movement at all – it was if we were still on the ground. I looked out my port, but all I saw was an increasingly dark sky.

The sensation of being on the ground seemed to last forever, but it actually lasted for only three minutes. At seventy-two kilometers above the ground, the capsule released its hold on the lift cable, and commenced its final eight-kilometer freefall to the skyport. My initial, completely unexpected, reaction was panic as all my weight disappeared. My body knew I was falling. Despite my intellect, every fiber in my being shouted *Falling... Falling!* To my embarrassment, my gorge rose in reaction. I swallowed hard to quell my stomach, and gripped my armrests fiercely as I fought to keep from hurling my stomach contents. After about a minute-and-a- half, I heard a clank as the capsule clamped to the frictionless motion deflector connecting the lift cable to the Amelia Earhart Skyport. I felt weight return, and my nausea completely disappeared as a gantry tilted us to horizontal.

To my amusement, I noticed that one of my guys actually did hurl – into a bag, fortunately.

Since the jump was to be from *Fred Noonan Skyport* over Jarvis Island, the plan called for us to transit right through *Amelia Earhart Skyport*, and ride the rail to *Noonan*. As our capsule glided into the capsule bay, the disembodied soft female voice we had heard earlier informed us that our seats would rotate 180 degrees for the reverse launch down the rail. Following that rotation, the gantry moved the capsule along the track with a slight jerk, and across to the rail. The capsule moved back against the kick thruster, where a clank signaled its successful attachment. Then the gantry gripping the capsule performed a half-turn, and the capsule shuddered slightly as the clamp attached a launch pouch. The disembodied voice commenced a short countdown.

"Five…four…three…two…one…zero…"

EQUATORIAL PACIFIC – FRED NOONAN SKYPORT (JARVIS ISLAND)

I felt myself pushed back into my seat with a very tolerable amount of g-force. It felt much like stepping hard on the accelerator of a car, and keeping it there for a while – eleven minutes, to be exact. Then a soft chime signaled the seat rotation just before the thruster ignited. I began to feel a bit uneasy with the realization that we were careening toward the skyport at several klicks per second, but the feeling vanished with the sound of the thruster. Almost immediately, I began to feel the deceleration as I was pushed back into my seat again. As before, the feeling was not uncomfortable. Before I had a chance to think much about the process, the deceleration lifted as the capsule glided into the bay at *Fred Noonan Skyport*.

Several clanks signaled removal of spent thruster and the launch pouch, and then the gantry moved the capsule to the bay where hydraulic rams created a seal with the lock, and the gull-wing doors lifted.

We disembarked into the skyport, where we were welcomed by the six-person duty shift. Their job was to deal with people and cargo, manhandle incoming and outgoing kick thrusters, and generally ensure that *Noonan Skyport* ran as designed. We spent a few minutes admiring the view from eighty klicks in the sky through the large polymer windows. I gotta tell you, it's damned impressive, any way you slice it. The horizon was out a thousand-ten klicks of empty ocean in every direction, except for two islands, Kiritimati – my destination – at 379 klicks on a northeasterly bearing, and Tabuaeran Atoll at 475 klicks slightly right of north. I thought I could see a smudge where Kiritimati should have been, but Tabuaeran was half-way to the horizon and invisible to the naked eye. The ocean was deep blue, covered by streaks of brilliant white cloud swirls in opposing patterns to the north and south. Oh yeah, there was one more island eighty klicks directly below us. The lower deck of the skyport boasted a large window that looked directly down on Jarvis. The Jarvis Skytower met the skyport right beside this window and rapidly disappeared toward the island below. From both decks, the fragile-appearing rail simply faded from view toward the west. And the sky above – oh my! The sky above was a deep black punctuated with more stars than I had ever seen. The Milky Way stretched from horizon to horizon, a brilliant band of countless multi-colored points of light. I had never experienced anything like it! I could have spent all day admiring the view.

True to the Socket Controller's word, a few minutes after we disembarked, the cargo capsule arrived carrying my Gryphon-7. Since we were there to do a job, Lt. Nelson pushed a bit, and we reluctantly stopped playing tourists, donned our helmets, checked comms, and – under the watchful eye of a female shift member – passed through the lock into the evacuated capsule arrival bay. The Lieutenant remained in the passenger area to brief the crew on what we were doing, and to keep control of what little security about the operation remained. Normally, hydraulic rams press a capsule to the lock seal so the gull-wing doors can open into the skyport. The cargo capsule, however, remained inside the bay so we could access the wing directly.

You have to remember that we were not there for publicity, for the most part anyway. We needed to test the limits of *Gryphon-7*. This was an entirely new kind of weapon, or perhaps *delivery system* is a better way to characterize it. It was imperative that we test its limits. We had to know its operational boundaries. That's why we were there. So, we pulled the rolled-up *Gryphon-7* from the cargo capsule, and laid it out for setup. Once the carapace had inflated, and the systems checked, two of the guys held it upright while I securely fastened the wide Velcro band across my middle. This was particularly important, because I would be hanging from these straps for the entire flight. I slipped my arms and legs through the retaining straps, and the guys tightened them. I could have done this myself, but it was much easier with help. I wrapped my hands around the grip controllers – I was ready.

Basically, the skyport capsule bay is an elongated cylinder with atmospheric seals at both ends. When we passed through the lock from the one-atmosphere skyport main deck, we entered what was virtually the vacuum of space. Lt. Nelson joined us after I was winged up and we were ready. He gave me a quick once-over – not that I needed it, but if something happened to me, it was his ass. Besides, I think he really cared for me and the rest of the guys. We walked along the rail through the open seal at the other end of the cylinder, the one the capsules pass through to catch the rail. Overhead, the capsule gantry waited silently for the next arriving capsule, that was probably sitting in the launch bay on Baker waiting for us to get the hell out of the way. We stepped onto a catwalk that looked like expanded metal, but was actually a special polymer that hardened under UV light to a strength many times greater than steel with a tiny fraction of its weight. In front of us, the rail in its casing looked unbelievably fragile. It seemed to hang in mid-air, I mean mid-space, suspended inside a twenty-meter-long one-and-a-half-meter-wide half- cylinder that extended several meters out from the skyport. It was constructed from the same light-weight material as the catwalk. We all attached safety lines from our suits to several anchor points on the catwalk, and then gingerly walked along the grate at the bottom of the horizontal half- cylinder.

It was an incredibly eerie feeling, knowing that there was nothing beneath me but eighty klicks of empty – well, I guess that at least half of that was air, technically, but it sure looked like empty, except for some fleecy clouds passing below. As you probably can guess, heights don't really bother me, so I had no problem standing right at the edge of the grate. Besides, I was still attached to my safety line.

I made sure of my orientation. The smudge that was Kiritimati Island lay 379 klicks over my right shoulder – and eighty down. One final Link check, and high-fives all around, although that's hard to do in a spacesuit with a *Gryphon-7* on my back, and I launched.

EQUATORIAL PACIFIC — GRYPHON FLIGHT

Howland, Baker, Jarvis & Kiribati Islands – Flight of the Gryphon

Immediately, I was in familiar territory, no different really from my 15,000-meter jump. I tumbled straight down, because there was no air to support me. No nausea, though; even my innards knew what was happening as I broke the tumble and staged myself horizontally. First, I extended my tail. "Tail extended and locked," I reported. My *Gryphon* was now two meters long. Next, I spread my wings to their full three-meter-wingspan. "Wings extended and locked," I reported, drily. "Rocket ignited, heading vector set to zero-four-niner-decimal-five-four, horizontal velocity two-hundred kph," I reported as I ignited my rocket, got myself pointed in the right direction, and gunned it until I reached my designated horizontal velocity.

With my house-keeping tasks out of the way, I relaxed against my straps, settled into my belly-band, and located my goal in the heads-up. I was dead on. I flattened myself as near to horizontal as possible, and then checked my drop rate. I caught my breath, and I imagine that my readouts in *Noonan* displayed a jump in heart-rate. I was plummeting downward at nearly Mach 1 and still accelerating – after only thirty seconds of freefall.

"Are you guys getting this?" I asked with a level of excitement that even I could hear.

"Piece of cake, Tiger," the Lieutenant drawled.

"Nothin' you ain't done before," the Senior Chief added. "Keep the chatter comin'!"

"I'm pushing Mach two, guys." I was passing sixty seconds. "No drag that I can feel."

Thirty seconds later, the Senior Chief said, "Your suit temp is way high. Can you feel it?"

"You're kiddin', right? I'm doing Mach two-point-four, ferchrissake... whaddya expect?" He was right, though, it was more than a little warm, but I was beginning to bite some air. I had fallen 40,000 meters and covered only five horizontal klicks thus far. Fortunately, my forward velocity was increasing as I grabbed more air.

I was tempted to kick in the rocket again, but the Lieutenant must have read my mind. "Conserve your fuel, Tiger," he told me. "We got your back."

I agreed, I guess. I had about twenty-five klicks of fuel left, and I really needed to save it for Kiritimati.

Remember, I could push myself for thirty klicks on rocket alone, but I had no idea what I might find at my goal, so he was right, I needed to conserve fuel. That meant no climbing under any circumstances, and no level flight either, if I wanted to have fuel when I got there. The increasing air resistance let me convert some of my downward velocity to lift. That, plus air drag actually slowed my fall to about half, so that as I passed 30,000 meters about thirty-six seconds later, I was falling at only about Mach 0.8.

You gotta see this in context. I was falling from 80,000 meters, just me and my *Gryphon*. If I did nothing, I would be a cooked piece of dead meat by the time I hit the water, but I had already done something. My fall speed was less than half of what it had been, and my forward velocity had increased to just short of 600 kph. This got me another six horizontal klicks and an *attaboy* from the Senior Chief. I was pretty busy right about then and had little time for conversation, but I grunted my appreciation. I still had a glide ratio of only one-to-two – one forward for every two down, which sucks, but I was gaining on it.

At this height I had a pretty good air bite, so that seventy-two seconds later I was falling through 20,000 meters at 500 kph with a glide ratio of about two-to-one, meaning my forward velocity was just about Mach 1.0. I had chewed up another twenty-four horizontal klicks. This is where I really started to grab air. I retained most of my forward velocity but dropped my descent to only fifty.

Twelve minutes later, I passed through 10,000 meters and had traveled a full 220 klicks closer to Kiritimati. That left 124 to go with 10,000 meters of air under me. My forward speed was now a relatively slow 250 with a full ten-to-one rate of descent of 20. That would get me 125 klicks, which left me a bonus klick plus another twenty-five under power. Things were looking pretty good right about then.

That's when Lt. Nelson commented wryly, "I concur with your numbers."

"So...I been talkin' in my sleep again," I said, and got a chuckle from the Senior Chief.

"Looks like we're picking up some weather ahead," the Lieutenant added. "Off to your right a bit."

I was cruising straight and true, and was passing through 5,000 meters with about seventy-five klicks left to fly, when I spotted it off to the right and ahead at about twenty degrees. It was what they call a tropical squall down on the water. These guys appear and disappear almost randomly. None of us saw this one coming. From where I was, however, a wall of cloud, cumulonimbus calvus actually, seemed to rise right out of the ocean to the east of Kiritimati to a height of about 3,000 meters. "Are you guys getting this?" I asked. Someone acknowledged – I'm not sure who.

As I moved forward, the squall's relative bearing to me did not change. "It looks like that sucker and I are going to collide right over Kiritimati," I said.

"Looks that way," the Lieutenant agreed.

"You can always ditch," the Senior Chief quipped, "if you think it's more than you can handle."

Even though his comments were half-jest, he was right. This was turning out not to be your normal squall, but rather the mother of all rapidly moving thunderstorms. I really did not want to be anywhere near that sonofabitch.

But that storm and I had an unavoidable meeting with destiny.

Worst case scenario, I thought to myself, *is that I got a kiss from Apryl before Mother Nature kicks my butt.*

"You have all the luck!" the Senior Chief said with a chuckle.

"Well, shit! Thinkin' out loud again," I said back. "Gotta stop doing that."

✷

Kiritimati is an elongated atoll about seventy-five klicks long and thirty at its widest, at an angle of about forty-five degrees west of north. From my aerial perspective, it occupied a swath of about forty klicks, which meant that when the storm and I rendezvoused over the island, I had no place to go. I suppose I could have ditched before the storm hit, as the Senior Chief had coyly suggested, but that seemed like a cop-out.

"I'm wearing a spacesuit, guys," I said. "So long as I don't crash, I should be okay."

"We're considering your options," Lt. Nelson said.

With just a few minutes left, and already feeling the effects of the storm, I decided to put my equipment to a full-bore test, no matter what the bosses said. After all, I was wearing a full spacesuit strapped to a *Gryphon-7*, and I was here – they were up there. "Screw it!" I said. "I'm doin' it!"

I pointed my rig at the storm's heart, powered the rocket for a few seconds, and plunged into the wall of cloud. Instantly, I lost all visual orientation, except the visual sensation that I was moving really fast through something.

"Talk to me!" Lt. Nelson said.

"Woo-oo," I answered as my twenty kph fall rate instantly changed to fifty kph rising, and my belly-band pressed hard against my midriff. I was accelerating upward rapidly. "You guys still with me?" I shouted, as the squall raged around me, soaking everything.

"We got you, Tiger!" That was Senior Chief Boldt.

A hundred seconds later, I was flung out of the top of the thunderhead, fully 3,000 meters over Kiritimati, and rising at 100 kph. The wet had turned to a layer of ice that began flaking off as I continued to rise. Below me, lightning played furiously between the thunderheads. "I still have twenty-five klicks of fuel, and now I got thirty of glide," I said, as I wrestled back full control of the *Gryphon* and cleared the top of the thunderhead that had vomited me into the sky. "Oops!" I hadn't intended to say that aloud. "I'm falling back in," I said as I found myself plunging headfirst back down into the lightning-filled inferno, trailing ice shards behind me.

"Trust your instruments," the Lieutenant said quietly to help me regain control.

I used a burst of fuel to force myself into a horizontal attitude, and oriented the *Gryphon* with the heads-up GPS. I was doing 250 and rising again. This time I exited the cloud top with more grace, heading northeast away from Kiritimati at 200 kph. Once again, I was covered with ice, and once again, I had a full thirty klicks of glide available. "I'm gonna swing a wide arc to the north and come in under the trailing edge of the storm," I commented. "I'll land nice-as-you-please at the edge of their airport runway." I was only about twenty klicks to the northeast at about 3,000 meters, so I had plenty of air. At least, that's how I had it figured.

"Where the fuck did that come from?" I didn't even see the airstream that captured me. One moment I was flying free and clear, looking for a good place to land, and the next I was slammed into the north wall of the squall, but this time, instead of rising, I was falling – fast. Things were happening very quickly, and I had no choice but to fire the rocket to stop my descent and gain some horizontal traction. The squall was petering out behind me as it passed Kiritimati, but I was fighting like hell to keep from crashing into the waves directly below. By the time I was back in control, Kiritimati was several klicks behind me to the east, and ahead of me, lay over 3,000 klicks of open ocean. "You guys still with me?" I panted, breathless from the heavy exertion. I whipped around, fired the rocket to maintain a five-meter-altitude, and took aim for the center of the island several klicks ahead of me.

"Yeah…nice save!" Senior Chief Boldt's voice was unemotional and calming.

KIRITIMATI ISLAND

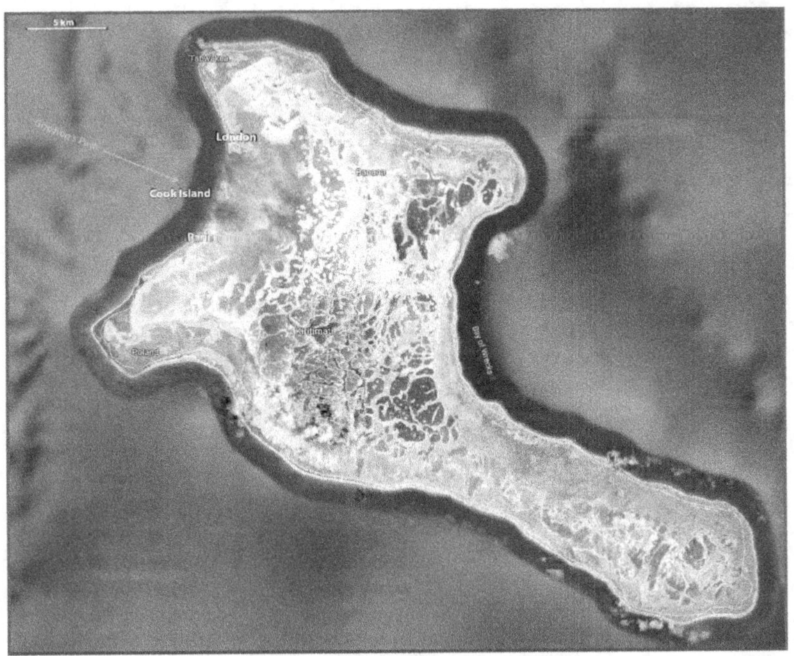

Kiritimati Island –Gryphon splashdown

My fuel gauge indicated five klicks of fuel remaining, but I had no reference for gauging the distance of a thirteen-meter-high atoll from five meters over the waves. Ahead of me I could see the open arms of the atoll embracing the inner lagoon, the tiny hamlet of London to the north and even smaller Paris about three klicks to the south. Directly between them lay uninhabited Cook Island – my immediate goal, I decided. And it could have been one or ten klicks away – I simply didn't know.

"Can I make Cook?" I asked.

"There's a chance," the Lieutenant said.

"By my reckoning," the Senior Chief added, "you're still three klicks out, but you only got two-and-a-half klicks of fuel." He paused. "Try flappin' your arms…"

The water beneath me shallowed noticeably as the wave tops grew higher. One-and-a-half minutes later, with me still beyond the breaker line about 200 meters from shore, the rocket coughed and quit. I hit the drink, unceremoniously, belly first.

"You okay, Tiger?" Senior Chief Boldt asked. "Fine," I said, "working my way ashore." The *Gryphon-7* was the best wingsuit I had ever flown, but it sucked as a surfboard, especially when I was face-down, strapped to the bottom. I retracted the tail and wings, unstrapped my hands and legs, and commenced an ungainly dogpaddle. It took a while, but I was finally just beyond the breaker line. I loosened the Velcro belly-band and pulled myself loose from the *Gryphon*. I grabbed it by the tail, pulled it underwater, and flipped it end-for-end.

"What's goin' on?" It was the Senior Chief.

"Goin' surfin'," I said. I pulled myself on top of the inverted *Gryphon*, knelt near the nose, and waited for the next big wave. I had to wait only about thirty seconds, and then I started paddling for all I was worth. The wave picked me up, and I started moving down its face. I jumped to my feet, set myself to a proper surfing stance, and pressed down with my back foot so the *Gryphon's* stabilizers took a bite. I turned left pretty-as-you-please, and glided at an angle down the eight-meter-high wave face…that is, for all of about two seconds, followed by a spectacular wipeout and a perfect over-the-falls tumble as the wave whipped both me and the *Gryphon* down to the sandy bottom, and then back up through the churning water column so we emerged behind the wave.

"You okay, Tiger?" The Senior Chief actually sounded concerned.

"Yeah – I'll tell you about it after. Pretty busy right now." I was watching the next wave and trying to get stomach-down flat on the upside-down *Gryphon* before it reached me.

This time I stayed flat, moving my hands just enough to get a bit of an angle on the wave face so I wouldn't plow into the bottom with the wave crest crashing over me. It wasn't very elegant, but I didn't wipeout. The *Gryphon* finally settled to the wet white sand as the wave receded. I wasted no time in grabbing the *Gryphon* and hurrying up the beach to where the sand was definitely dry.

"Status report!" It was Lt. Nelson. I briefed him on the final wet fifteen minutes of my flight, and made some suggestions for dealing with future water entries. They were mostly about stability in the water and a means of powered propulsion. It was only a few minutes later that a Zodiac with four SEALS from the second squad arrived on the lagoon side of Cook Island.

DAEDALUS – FINALE

I'm sure you know the rest of the story, so I won't repeat it here. I survived, and then I survived my fifteen minutes of fame. My *Gryphon-7* hangs in the Smithsonian, but you know that, too.

The Jarvis drop has been accomplished probably a hundred times since then, but mine was the one with all the excitement. We've moved on to bigger and better things now, and have our sights set on a drop from low-earth- orbit. I'll let you know when it finally happens.

PLEASE POST A REVIEW FOR DAEDALUS

ON

AMAZON.COM AND GOODREADS.COM

I really appreciate you posting a review on Amazon and Goodreads. Posting to Amazon.com is intuitive. To post a review on Goodreads.com, click on this link, or go to their website, and become a member if you are not already one. Search for *Daedalus*, and click on the "Want to read" button under the image of *Daedalus*. Indicate that you have read *Daedalus* and then you will be able to post a review. Thank you very much for going through this effort!

Excerpt from the First Chapter of: SLINGSHOT

by

Robert G. Williscroft

EQUATORIAL PACIFIC – SOUTHEAST OF BAKER ISLAND

Margo stopped kicking her feet as the ominous gray shapes flashed into her peripheral view. Long, tawny hair floated past her head as her feet dropped below her slim, brightly clad body. She took a deep breath and floated slightly upward. A hint of fear crept into her mind as she turned toward three gray, sleek predators cruising just inside the limit of her vision, about twenty-five meters away.

A gentle touch on her shoulder startled her. She turned to see Alex Regent tapping the depth reading on his dive- console with his index finger. Margo reached down and grasped her console, turning it so she could read her depth: twenty-five meters. She had drifted upward five meters since seeing the sharks.

Margo exhaled angrily and let some air out of her breathing bag. She knew better than to lose track of her depth. Out there, her life depended on a constant awareness of exactly how deep she was. Together she and Alex sank back to thirty meters. Off to their right, the three gray shapes drifted with them. Would she ever get used to it, she thought, as she released a bit of air into her bag to stop her descent.

"Alex," she said.

There was no response.

"Alex!" She tapped the back of her console several times.

"Alex!" Nothing but silence.

Alex placed himself in front of Margo and looked into her facemask. With his right hand, he formed a circle with thumb and forefinger. His three other fingers extended straight up.

Margo returned the sign indicating she was all right while nodding vigorously. Then she pointed to her ear and lifted her console, tapping the back. Alex fumbled at his ear, and then tapped his console, and then shook his head.

Great, Margo thought, *EFCom is busted just when we really need it. Not busted,* she corrected herself, *just a submerged antenna*. She pointed to the three menacing shapes off to her right. Alex turned and scanned around them. Above and just behind them the blue-painted hull of their boat bobbed in the gentle waves. About twenty meters ahead of them hung a smooth, horizontal fluorescent orange tube about one meter in diameter. To the left, it stretched into the gloom; to the right, it angled downward. The fluorescent tube was attached to a slender cable angling up to the shadow of a buoy just beneath the surface to their right. Alex turned back toward Margo, making an exaggerated shrug.

Margo reached for her dive-console again and pressed a button located prominently on its face. The three sharks turned and commenced a meandering movement toward the two divers. Their front fins extended stiffly downward at about forty-five degrees. Their backs arched slightly, and their blunt snouts moved back and forth as they approached.

Margo felt her hair stand up on the nape of her neck.

She turned to Alex and motioned him to her side. Alex withdrew a telescoped baton from its holder at his waist and extended it to its full one-and-a-half-meter length. He checked the safety lever near its handle, and with his thumb, he flicked the lever so it pointed forward. As the sharks drew nearer, he held the stick out in front of him, pointed in their direction. Margo glanced around them again and pushed her console button once more. Alex waved the stick about slowly and then steadied up on the nearest of the three menacing monsters.

Suddenly, with blurring speed, the nearest shark attacked. Alex struck out with his stick, the jolt of its impact rocking him backward. A sharp crack was followed by a hissing sound as carbon dioxide rushed into the shark's body. In the same moment, flashes of silvery- black streaked from several directions. One of the remaining sharks was struck broadside by a dolphin's blunt nose. In a flash, it disappeared.

The animal Alex had injected rolled on its side and began a crazed, uncontrolled spiral toward the surface thirty meters above them. On its way up, it was hit several times by charging dolphins. It expired of massive embolisms before reaching fifteen meters. In the melee, the third shark vanished.

Margo reached out for Alex, grabbed a handful of breathing bag, and pulled him close to her. She placed the flat of her full-facemask against his and looked deeply into his eyes, as close to a kiss as she could come under the circumstances. Even down here, they were deep blue.

Several bubbles escaped from the positive pressure maintained inside their masks and shimmered their way toward the surface, expanding rapidly as they rose.

Like an old-time scuba diver, Margo thought, watching the rising silvery spheres. Instinctively she checked the volume in her breathing bag and glanced at the gauge on her tiny, ultra-high-pressure air flask. She found she was holding her breath, and as she felt the need to breathe, a gentle pressure developed against her back. She pulled back and turned to confront a two-and-a-half-meter-long dolphin nudging her from behind.

It was one of four that had responded to her sonic signal – George, her favorite. The other three dolphins crowded in around the neoprene and nylon suited divers, jostling each other for attention. Margo rubbed the head dome of each and indicated to Alex that he should do the same. Then the two of them turned their attention back to the tube suspended in front of them.

Alex swam to the angled portion and began to search along the tube's length, descending slowly. Margo dropped her arm from George's neck and kicked in Alex's direction, keeping him in sight, but staying between him and the surface. The four cetaceans arrowed toward the surface and grabbed a gulp of air, then settled back down, playfully cycling between Alex and Margo, gently jostling them. About thirty minutes later, Alex motioned Margo to join him. She released a bubble of air from her bag and dropped down beside him. Her console showed a depth of fifty meters. Alex pointed to a five-centimeter rip in the bottom curve of the tube's fluorescent covering.

Margo reached into a deep pocket located on the left leg of her suit and withdrew a role of patching tape. Alex stretched the edges of the tear, and Margo applied a strip of self-sealing tape along the opening. Then she located a small pneumatic valve on the top of the tube and attached a hose from her spare air tank. On a signal from Alex, she released air into the tube, forcing water out through a one- way valve on the underside. She stopped when bubbles escaped from the lower valve.

As the tube rose slowly, Margo held on, keeping track of their progress on her console. They stopped rising when the gauge read thirty meters. Margo felt the tube – it was taut and solid. She tapped the back of her console, listening for the faint rush of sound in her ears. Nothing. She pointed to the back of her console and then her ear, and shook her head. Alex offered another of his exaggerated underwater shrugs and grinned, although the only part of the grin she could see was his crinkled eyes. She grinned back and pointed toward the suspension buoy and their boat, making an angled upward sign with her free hand. Alex nodded, checked his console, and they both headed back, slowly rising as they swam.

Margo saw Alex check his console from time to time, making certain they kept below the ever-changing ceiling limit it calculated for him. Since she had remained shallower than Alex for most of the dive, she knew she would be safe following his lead. She looked around at the four dolphins. Her earlier fright was gone, and she simply enjoyed George's protective nearness and the playful bumps and nudges from the others.

On the surface finally, Alex dropped his facemask down around his neck, fully inflated his bag and grinned at Margo. "Close call down there!"

Margo shoved her facemask down and patted the glistening snout that appeared in front of her. "Thanks, George. I love you too."

The dolphin mewed a pleased response, lifted his body out of the water and backed away, chattering as he went.

The other three animals circled at and below the surface, keeping watch over their human charges.

"What happened to the EFCom?" Margo asked. "I expected it to come back online as soon as the antenna surfaced."

"Broken antenna wire, I imagine," Alex answered. "Storm damage, I'm sure," said Margo, as they turned

and headed toward the waiting vessel.

"Probably," agreed Alex. "But that wasn't a burst seam," he added.

"Yeah, maybe the sinking tube snapped the wire."

Actually, tube flotation chambers flooded on a regular basis. They had patched a full ten percent of them since the project started. But it was a bit unusual to find a rip on the tube bottom, and the Electrostatic Field Communication ("EFCom") transceivers on the buoys almost always survived.

✷

The EFCom buoy nearest the tear had ceased transmitting, and the buoys on either side of the tear had signaled their departure from datum a day earlier. Alex had opted to employ an electrostatic field communication system, because of its clear underwater signal transmission capability that was independent of acoustic conditions, since it didn't rely on sound transmission through the water. Every buoy, each skimmer and floater, and every diver was outfitted with one of the small EFCom transceivers. Alex had inspected the non-transmitting buoy personally during an overflight from Jarvis Island. There was nothing visible on the two kilometers of surface between the buoys; they were closer together, but not so that it was visible to the eye. Nevertheless, the remaining 1,828-odd buoy-suspended kilometers of tube were stressing from the downward pull of the waterlogged section. The buoy near the tear was several meters underwater.

Suspended inside the flotation tube were two virtually impervious, lightweight, hose-like tubes, each about six centimeters in diameter, called vacuum sheaths. Two shallow channels jutted out from the bottom of each vacuum sheath, filled with electronically controlled suspending magnets. Magnetically suspended inside each vacuum sheath was a five-centimeter tube of segmented soft iron officially called the rotor, but more popularly known as the ribbon, so named from the earliest conceptions back in the 1980s of the Launch Loop inventor, Keith Lofstrom. Alex was eager to check continuity readings to make certain the vacuum sheaths had not breached. They were not yet evacuated, but seawater entry at this stage would seriously delay the entire project. If the EFCom had not crapped out, the tests would already be underway.

Alex glanced ahead at Margo Jackson, cavorting with her four dolphins as they made their leisurely way back to the waiting boat. His field engineer in charge of underwater construction was a remarkable female. Nearly as tall as his own 183 centimeters, her model's slender figure, encased in electric-blue nylon-covered neoprene, seemed to lack feminine curves. He knew differently, of course, having joined her bikini-clad person from time to time for morning swims since the project began over two years ago.

The project – Alex had lived with it for three years before actual construction began. Longer, actually, if you considered dreams – since before the incredible, worldwide bi-millennial celebration when he still was a young boy.

There was the nearly simultaneous publication in America and England of practically identical ideas in 1985. Paul Birch published an article in *The Journal of the British Interplanetary Society*, while in America Keith Lofstrom published his article in a supplement to *The Journal of the Astronautical Sciences*, he recalled. Nobody could agree on the names: Skyrail, Launch Loop, Beanstalk. There were others, but the idea is what counted, the sky-shaking idea that you don't need rockets to get into space.

Newspapers were full of explanations three-and-a-half years ago when the aging president of a computer software giant made the announcement. He would funnel a significant portion of company profits into the consortium. Space travel would become as commonplace and inexpensive as the personal computers his pioneering work had made possible. He went on to outline the easy-to- understand concept.

Imagine a water hose streaming water in a parabolic arch. Deflect the water and funnel it back to the start through a pump, creating a closed system. Make the stream strong enough and the hose light enough, and the entire structure will support itself – the water holding up the hose structure. Now, replace the water with a thin, closed-loop pipe of segmented soft iron. Make it 5,000 kilometers around and accelerate it to orbital velocity with gigantic linear induction motors from two points on the equator 2,000 kilometers apart. The center section of the structure, including both the outgoing and return legs of the loop, will rise to about eighty kilometers above the Earth. Supply access to the upstream end in space with a Kevlar-hung elevator, and you can launch capsules by magnetically coupling them to the rapidly moving pipe of iron.

Slingshot, they called it. The greatest engineering undertaking in the history of the world, they said.

As the on-scene project manager, Alex was responsible for getting the job done, on schedule, on budget. He was building a gossamer structure over 2,500 kilometers long, a frail spider web, completely invisible when viewed from more than a few kilometers. Alex grinned wryly. All *Slingshot* really consisted of was a fancy evacuated tube, a flexible iron pipe, four linear drivers and their power sources, some guy wires, and a couple of elevators. Put that way it seemed simple enough. But, of course, it wasn't simple at all, and for all his skill and engineering competence, and despite surface appearances, deep down Alex was not entirely sure that he could make it happen.

Margo and Alex climbed up the ladder and onto *Skimmer One's* bobbing fantail. This was one of two skimmers on the project – twelve-meter-long surface-effect boats that looked more like a floating aircraft than a traditional motorboat. They were capable of 200 knots, skimming about one-and-a-half meters over the wave tops. They had a small open fantail, just large enough for a couple of divers to doff their gear. Being on the fantail when the skimmer was on its cushion was more than dangerous, and was strictly prohibited throughout the project.

Alex signaled to the waiting coxswain, and they got underway for Baker, plowing through the water while Alex and Margo remained exposed. He and Margo stood near the stern railing and removed their dripping skins. Alex looked back at the buoys, now presumably in their proper places.

"How many more times?" Alex looked quizzically at Margo.

"Who knows?" She glanced back at the bobbing buoys. "We have repair people available at both ends. We shouldn't be doing this ourselves, you know." She turned and looked directly at Alex. "What do you think – weather or sabotage?"

Alex shrugged and tossed the spent carbon dioxide cartridge from his shark stick in the general direction of the cavorting dolphins. "I wanted to see for myself, and I still don't know. Does it matter? We can't patrol the entire eighteen-hundred-twenty-eight-kilometer length anyway."

"What are we dealing with?" Margo asked. "You don't get out here in a rowboat."

"We're two thousand wet klicks from any kind of civilization," Alex said. "At minimum, that's a large motor- yacht or even an ocean sailer – you know, one of those we maybe can afford when this job is done." He sighed. "We're dealing with lots of money and someone with a major bitch."

He looked into her green eyes.

"Just keep my tubes at depth." His blue eyes flashed, and he turned toward the cockpit to radio his orders to test pipe continuity.

✸

Margo dropped her eyes at his challenge. For the thousandth time, she asked herself if she had bitten off more than she could chew with this assignment. Was it her fault that the flotation chambers kept ripping? Was she missing something important? Was she copping out to imply there might have been sabotage? And yet, Alex seemed to agree that it might be sabotage. When she joined the project two years ago, the newspapers had acclaimed her as the ideal role model for the new twenty-first-century woman. At times that burden lay heavily on her shoulders, as it did now, she reflected.

It was a vast responsibility, and there was no way one person actually could control all of it at once. How Alex handled the weight of the entire project awed her, but she was careful never to let him know.

Margo watched Alex step into the cockpit. He was tall and slender, richly tanned from his constant outdoor work. She felt a softness well up inside her, a gentle warmth spreading out from the pit of her stomach. She bit her lower lip and turned angrily to lean on the after-railing.

None of that, she chided herself. This assignment was too important, and the stakes too high, to let any kind of emotion intrude. As she entered the cabin and sealed the port, the skipper switched modes, and pressurized air quickly filled the hard-sided skirt. In moments the skimmer lifted out of the water, except for the port and starboard skirts that protruded about a meter into the waves. Within seconds, high-pressure water nozzles jetted water from the end of each skirt, and within thirty seconds *Skimmer One* was approaching 200 knots.

As *Skimmer One* headed into the afternoon sun, trailing an arrow-straight wake of white foam, Margo stood looking aft through the sealed port, remembering her instinctive sharing, and their underwater kiss following the fright of nearly becoming shark food. She shook off the sensation and busied herself with putting away their diving equipment. But a hint of a smile remained on her lips as they shot over the surface, finally settling back onto the water as they entered the small protected artificial harbor on the west side of Baker Island, just south of a shallow reef that went dry at low tide.

You have just been reading from Chapter One of Slingshot, the 1st book, in The Starchild Trilogy, Robert Williscroft's exciting Science Fiction trilogy.

WORDS OF PRAISE FOR SLINGSHOT

Slingshot does for the launch loop what Arthur C. Clarke's *The Fountains of Paradise* or Sheffield's *Web Between the Worlds* did for the space elevator. Again, Williscroft delivers a great mix of hard science fiction and action.

— Alastair Mayer
Author of the *T-Space Series*

Robert Williscroft deftly crafts an energetic story around a phenomenal technological development just over the horizon: the space launch loop. The technical detail woven into this story is an education unto itself. But don't assume that Williscroft chooses raw infodump over story – *Slingshot* is an adventure that pulls you in, gives you characters that are engaging, and invites you to follow them through their challenges. What Williscroft has done in *Slingshot* is no easy task – he has balanced the *hard* aspect of science fiction with the character portrayals that those who despise that very *hard* science fiction beg for. The last decade has seen impressive leaps in the theoretical work toward the launch loop – this book couldn't come too soon! And you won't be able to keep from reading all the way to the end. Williscroft's art continues to be praise-worthy!

— Jason D. Batt, *100 Year Starship*
Author of *The Tales of Dreamside series*

I've been a fan of Robert Williscroft's books for a while now. They're action-packed and filled with all kinds of interesting, real-world information. *Slingshot* fits right in.

Slingshot is about the development of an earth-bound spaceport in which spaceships are taken 80 kilometers above the Earth by elevator and hurled onto their trajectory by a very fast moving ribbon of soft iron. It is much easier, cheaper, and cleaner to launch spaceships from here due to the rarified atmosphere. This concept may be a reality someday. The book begins with a foreword by Keith Lofstrom, the originator of this concept called the "launch loop."

Learning about the launch loop is the most interesting aspect of this novel. Williscroft's descriptions of the construction techniques, its operations, and the benefits for space travel are absolutely fascinating. The book takes place about thirty years in the future, and I could easily see such a project becoming a reality in that time.

The plot of the novel is driven by the development and construction of the project, which is being a threatened by ill-informed environmentalists bent on destroying the project. The launch loop is far greener than the current method of launching vehicles into space, but a sinister power has misled the environmentalists into believing that sabotaging the launch loop is saving the planet. Meanwhile, the sinister power is protecting its own economic interests.

As usual, Williscroft has a created a cast of interesting and driven characters. The book is a fascinating read, and you are guaranteed not only to learn a lot, but to dream about the future of space travel.

Marc Weitz, Past President
The Los Angeles Adventurers' Club

ABOUT THE AUTHOR

Dr. Robert G. Williscroft served twenty-three years in the U.S. Navy and the National Oceanic and Atmospheric Administration (NOAA). He commenced his service as an enlisted nuclear Submarine Sonar Technician in 1961, was selected for the Navy Enlisted Scientific Education Program in 1966, and graduated from University of Washington in Marine Physics and Meteorology in 1969. He returned to nuclear submarines as the Navy's first Poseidon Weapons Officer. Subsequently, he served as Navigator and Diving Officer on both catamaran mother vessels for the Deep Submergence Rescue Vehicle. Then he joined the Submarine Development Group One out of San Diego as the Officer-in-Charge of the Test Operations Group, conducting "deep-ocean surveillance and data acquisition" – which forms the basis for his Cold War novel *Operation Ivy Bells*.

In NOAA Dr. Williscroft directed diving operations throughout the Pacific and Atlantic. As a certified diving instructor for both the National Association of Underwater Instructors (NAUI) and the Multinational Diving Educators Association (MDEA), he taught over 3,000 individuals both basic and advanced SCUBA diving. He authored four diving books, developed the first NAUI drysuit course, developed advanced curricula for mixed gas and other specialized diving modes, and developed and taught a NAUI course on the Math and Physics of Advanced Diving. His doctoral dissertation for California Coast University, *A System for Protecting SCUBA Divers from the Hazards of Contaminated Water* was published by the U.S.

Department of Commerce and distributed to Port Captains worldwide. He also served three shipboard years in the high Arctic conducting scientific baseline studies, and thirteen months at the geographic South Pole in charge of National Science Foundation atmospheric projects.

Dr. Williscroft has written extensively on terrorism and related subjects. He is the author of a popular book on current events published by Pelican Publishing: *The Chicken Little Agenda – Debunking Experts' Lies*, now in its second edition as an eBook, and a new children's book series, *Starman Jones*, in collaboration with Dr. Frank Drake, world famous director of the Carl Sagan Center for the Study of Life in the Universe and the SETI Institute.

Dr. Williscroft's first novel in *The Starchild Trilogy, Slingshot*, tells the story of the construction of the world's first Space Launch Loop. *Slingshot* was launched at the Seattle International Space Elevator Conference in August, 2015. His second novel in *The Starchild Trilogy, The Starchild Compact,* is based on the discovery that Saturn's moon Iapetus is actually a derelict starship, and how Earth explorers eventually meet with the "Founders," who originally arrived on the starship and populated the Earth long ago. The third book in *The Starchild Trilogy, The Iapetus Federation*, tells the story of fanatical terrorist Saeed Ismail resurfacing following the dramatic events of *The Starchild Compact* to lead a global Jihad that leaves Earth in chaos. The Israelis, led by Founder Asshur, and what is left of the United States, led by Texas Governor Sam Houston, seek to escape the planet, and new technology being developed by Solar-System-wide Iapetus Federation may be the key to a successful exodus. The question is, will it be ready before Earth has sunk irrevocably into medieval barbarism? And if so, could it help the Federation expand even beyond the Solar System?

Dr. Williscroft is an active member of the venerable Adventurers' Club of Los Angeles, where he is the former Editor of the Club's monthly magazine. He is the current editor of the Colorado Authors' League monthly *InPrint*. He lives in Centennial, Colorado, with his wife, Jill, whom he met upon his return from the South Pole in 1982 and finally married in 2011, and their twin college boys (when they are home from school).

OTHER WORKS BY ROBERT G. WILLISCROFT

Please visit Amazon.com to discover other eBooks by Robert Williscroft and your favorite online or Brick & Mortar bookseller for their paper versions:

Current events:

The Chicken Little Agenda – Debunking "Experts'" Lies

Children's books:

The Starman Jones Series:

Starman Jones: A Relativity Birthday Present

Starman Jones Goes to the Dogs (scheduled for release in 2019)

Short Stories:

SWIC History:

Daedalus (scheduled for release in 2019)

Daedalus – LEO (scheduled for release in 2019)

Daedalus – Squad (scheduled for release in 2019)

Daedalus – Combat (scheduled for release in 2019)

Novels:

Mac McDowell Missions

Operation Ivy Bells

Operation Snow Cone (Scheduled for release 2019)

The Starchild Trilogy:

Slingshot

The Starchild Compact

The Iapetus Federation

The Oort Chronicles:

Icicle – A Tensor Matrix (scheduled for release in 2019)

The Oort – Interstellar Consequences (scheduled for release in 2020)

Oort Andromeda – Galactic Diaspora (scheduled for release in 2020)

CONNECT WITH ROBERT G. WILLISCROFT

Connect With

Robert G. Williscroft

I really appreciate you reading my book! Here are my social media coordinates:

Friend me on Facebook: https://www.facebook.com/robert.williscroft

Follow me on Twitter: *@RGWilliscroft*

Like my Amazon author page: *http://www.amazon.com/Robert-G.- Williscroft/e/B001JP52AS*

Subscribe to my blog: Thrawn Rickle

Connect on LinkedIn: *http://www.linkedin.com/in/argee/*

Visit my website: *http://robertwilliscroft.com*

Find me at my publisher's website: *FreshInkGroup.com/author/robertwilliscroft*

DAEDALUS GLOSSARY

Atoll – A ring-shaped reef, island, or chain of islands formed of coral.

Baker Compound – The *Slingshot* facility on Baker Island.

BUDS – Basic Underwater Demolition/SEAL training.

Cumulonimbus calvus – A moderately tall cumulonimbus cloud which is capable of precipitation, but has not yet reached the tropopause.

Cumulonimbus cloud – Thunderhead cloud.

CYA – Cover your ass.

Deflector – A series of permanent and electro-magnets that bend the path of the rapidly moving iron ribbon.

EMT – Emergency Medical Technician.

ETA – Estimated time of arrival.

Gryphon –A wingsuit-like carapace strapped on the body. It stopped short of the feet, but in flight could extend to a full two meters, stretching beyond the feet. It attached to the legs and arms, with special controls for each hand, and had a broad Velcro band across the midriff. It had extensible delta wings with a three-meter wingspan. The back end contained a small steerable hypergolic rocket engine, and the left and right wings each contained pressurized hypergolic fuel components. Switches in the hand units controlled the fuel valves. The Gryphon had a heads-up display with height-over-ground, airspeed, groundspeed, compass, and GPS coordinates superimposed on a map, plus various system readouts.

Gyrostabilizer – A gyroscopic device for maintaining the equilibrium of something such as a ship, aircraft, or spacecraft.

Howland Island – A coral island in the equatorial Pacific about sixty- five kilometers north of Baker Island. It was the destination of Amelia Earhart when she disappeared.

Hypergolic fuel– Fuel that ignites spontaneously when the individual fuel elements come into contact.

Hypergolic rocket– A rocket that uses hypergolic fuel.

Jarvis Compound – The *Slingshot* facility on Jarvis Island.

Keith Lofstrom – Inventor of the Launch Loop.

Kick thruster – A small, reigniteable solid-state rocket attached to a capsule, used for vector changes after release from the rail, or to slow down a capsule used to transit from Baker to Jarvis.

Klick – Slang word for kilometer.

Launch Loop – A means for getting into space without using rockets.

Launch Loop International – The company that and manages Slingshot.

Launch pouch – Attaches to the capsule underside, enabling magnetic acceleration of the capsule by the rail.

Mach number – The ratio of the speed of a body to the speed of sound in the surrounding medium.

Maglev train – A magnetically levitated train; it floats above the track propelled by magnetism.

Rail – Common term for the portion of the launch loop between the skyports.

Ribbon – Common term for the soft-iron tube that is the heart of the launch loop.

SEAL – An acronym for *Sea Air and Land*; a member of a Naval Special Warfare unit trained for unconventional warfare.

Skyport – The structure at the top of the skytower.

Skyrail – An alternative name for a Space Elevator or Launch Loop.

Skytower – The elevator-like set of cables that extends from the Skyport to the island below.

Slingshot – The Space Launch Loop between Baker and Jarvis Islands in the equatorial Pacific.

Socket – The attachment point on the island for the skytower.

SPELCO – Special Parachute and Logistics Consortium

Stratosphere – The second major layer of Earth's atmosphere, just above the troposphere.

Suspensor cable – A cable to which the skytower cable and double-lift cables are attached. It carries the weight of all the cables.

SWIC – SEAL Winged Insertion Command

Tensioner – A cable attached to the rail or downslopes and the ocean bottom, with a dynamic device that increases or decreases the tension as necessary to maintain Launch Loop stability.

Tropopause – The interface between the troposphere and the stratosphere.

Troposphere – The lowest region of the atmosphere, extending from the earth's surface to a height of about 6–10 km, which is the lower boundary of the stratosphere.

UV light – Ultra violet light.

Wingsuit –Aa suit with fabric filling the gaps between stretched out arms and ankles, and between the legs, enabling the wearer to glide through the air.

Fresh Ink Group

Independent Multi-media Publisher

Fresh Ink Group / Push Pull Press

❧

Hardcovers
Softcovers
All Ebook Platforms
Audiobooks
Worldwide Distribution

❧

Indie Author Services
Book Development, Editing, Proofing
Graphic/Cover Design
Video/Trailer Production
Website Creation
Social Media Management
Writing Contests
Writers' Blogs
Podcasts

❧

Authors
Editors
Artists
Experts
Professionals

❧

FreshInkGroup.com
info@FreshInkGroup.com
Twitter: @FreshInkGroup
Facebook.com/FreshInkGroup
LinkedIn: Fresh Ink Group

Fresh Ink Group

Also by Robert G. Williscroft

THE STARCHILD TRILOGY begins with building a Space Launch Loop enabling massive movement off Earth and subsequent settlement of Cislunar-Space, Mars, and beyond. SLINGSHOT is the story of the struggle behind constructing the largest machine ever built stretching between Baker and Jarvis Islands in the Equatorial Pacific, and how the men and women behind Slingshot overcome the project's physical, economic, and human obstacles. In THE STARCHILD COMPACT, a team exploring Saturn's moon Iapetus discovers it to be a derelict starship, and meets the Founders, remnants of an ancient, advanced race, the Ectarians, that arrived in the Solar System 150,000 years ago. Together, they create the Starchild Institute governed by a document they call the Starchild Compact to further develop and introduce Ectarian technology to the Solar System. Using Ectarian technology, they develop near lightspeed spacecraft, artificial wormholes, FTL starships, and human longevity. As human colonies expand into the Solar System, they form a governing coalition: THE IAPETUS FEDERATION. While a united Islam pursues a global Jihad that rages across the planet putting millions to the sword, the Federation enables an exodus from Earth using artificial wormholes. From hand-to-hand combat in the oceans, to battles on Earth's surface, to the challenge of living off-Earth and reaching for the stars, our heroes fight to survive and to expand humankind to the far reaches of the universe.

Find Robert at www.argee.net

www.ingramcontent.com/pod-product-compliance
Lightning Source LLC
Chambersburg PA
CBHW070453170726
48291CB00005B/1736

* 9 7 8 1 9 4 7 8 6 7 5 6 7 *